Swim!

BY EVE RICE
PICTURES BY MARISABINA RUSSO

 Greenwillow Books, New York

Gouache paints were used for the full-color art.
The text type is Geometric 706 Medium.

Text copyright © 1996 by Eve Rice
Illustrations copyright © 1996 by Marisabina Russo Stark
Printed in Hong Kong by South China Printing Company (1988) Ltd.
First Edition   10 9 8 7 6 5 4 3 2 1

Library of Congress Cataloging-in-Publication Data

Rice, Eve.
Swim! / by Eve Rice ; pictures by Marisabina Russo.
p.   cm.
Summary: A young girl describes all the things that she and her father
do when they go to the swimming pool each Saturday morning.
ISBN 0-688-14274-5 (trade).   ISBN 0-688-14275-3 (lib. bdg.)
[1. Swimming—Fiction.   2. Fathers and daughters—Fiction.]
I. Russo, Marisabina, ill.   II. Title.   PZ7.R3622Sw   1996   [E]—dc20
95-25081   CIP   AC

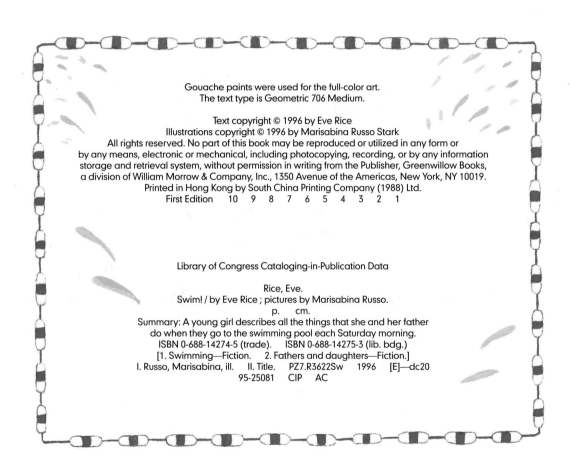

For Nate and Julie
and Beth, with love

—E. R.

For my helpers, James, Danielle, and Joe,
and for my own swimmers,
Sam, Ben, and Hannah

—M. R.

Every Saturday morning my dad and I go swimming—
just the two of us.
We pack our things to take to the pool in a big blue bag.
This is what I put in the bag:
   A bathing suit.
   A towel.
   A pool cap and a comb.
My dad asks, "All set?"
And I nod my head. So we are ready to go.

The pool is big, and it's indoors.

Lots of people are there already.

My dad and I put on our suits.

He helps me tuck my hair into my cap.

The cold water tickles my toes.
My dad jumps in and calls, "Come on!"
So I get in, up to my knees.
Then I close my eyes and push off the step—
straight to my dad.

I can dog-paddle and float on my back. I can hold my breath under the water.

"We are fish," my dad says, and we both laugh. Then we put our heads in the water and blow bubbles through our noses.

Where the water is shallow, I can stand and
throw a ball.
My dad throws it high in an arc. "Catch!"
And then I throw it back to him.
He gets it every time.

But the best part is when he teaches me to dive—my kind of dive.

"Like this," my dad says, as I hook my toes over the edge.

And he counts, "One, two, three . . . jump!"

He holds my hands, and then—with a splash—I jump in.

"That's great." He laughs. "Let's do it again."

I scramble out and do it again—at least a dozen times.

The last thing we always do is practice kicking.
"Bet you can't kick like me," my dad says. And
we each try to kick the hardest.
We kick and kick and kick—until we are too
tired to kick anymore.

"That's enough for today," he says.
My dad wraps me up in a big warm towel
as I get out.
And when we're dressed, we hurry home.

My mom opens the door and gives us each a hug.
"Tell me," she says, "how was your swim?"
So I tell her all about playing catch and being fish
and learning how to dive.

"You've had quite a morning," she says. "But now it's time for lunch."
We hang our suits and towels to dry by the kitchen door.

"I love to swim," I tell my mom as I sit down.
"I know," she says, and nods her head. "You and
   your dad are my favorite fish—my very own fish—
   so I am not surprised."
Then I look at my dad, and he winks at me.
And we both smile.